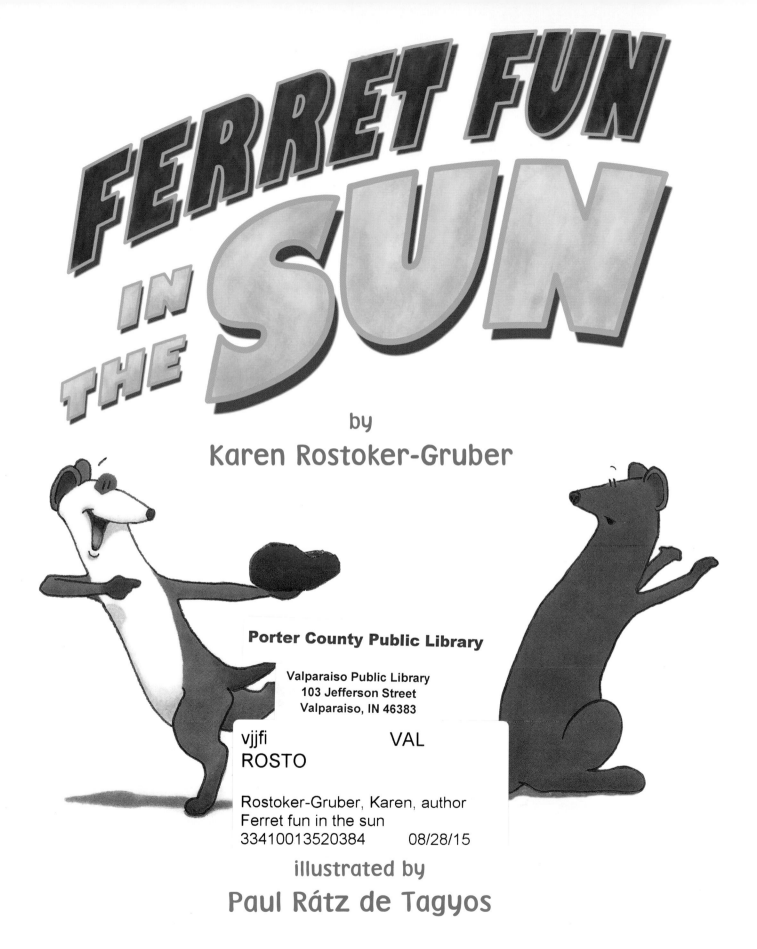

FERRET FUN IN THE SUN

by

Karen Rostoker-Gruber

illustrated by

Paul Rátz de Tagyos

two lions

two lions

Published by Two Lions, New York
www.apub.com

Amazon, the Amazon logo, and Two Lions are
trademarks of Amazon.com, Inc., or its affiliates.

Library of Congress Control Number: 2014943822

ISBN-13: 9781477826317 (hardcover)
ISBN-10: 1477826319 (hardcover)
ISBN-13: 9781477827581 (paperback)
ISBN-10: 1477827587 (paperback)

The illustrations are rendered in ink and marker.
Book design by Vera Soki

Printed in China
First Edition

For Bandit—fur-ever in our hearts.

This book is also dedicated to my daughter, Michelle,
who asked me to write a book about ferrets,
and to Laura Goforth, a park ranger
from Grand Canyon National Park.
—K.R-G.

Thanks to K R-G (as usual).
A very special thanks to Caitlin.
And to Anna . . . just 'cause.
—P.R.D.T.

"Fudge, Einstein, we're going to Arizona," said Andrea.

Andrea put their traveling cage in her car.

She's driving so fast my hammock won't stop rocking.

Just go to sleep. When you wake up, we'll be there.

A few hours later, Andrea carried their cage
into her room at the South Rim Ranch.

Andrea put their cage down. "I'm going to meet a friend.
I'll be back soon," she said. "Here are some treats."

After Einstein ate his treats, he slunk out
of his hammock and opened the cage door.

Einstein scampered away and started
exploring under the coffee table,

behind the curtains,

and up the sofa to the window ledge.

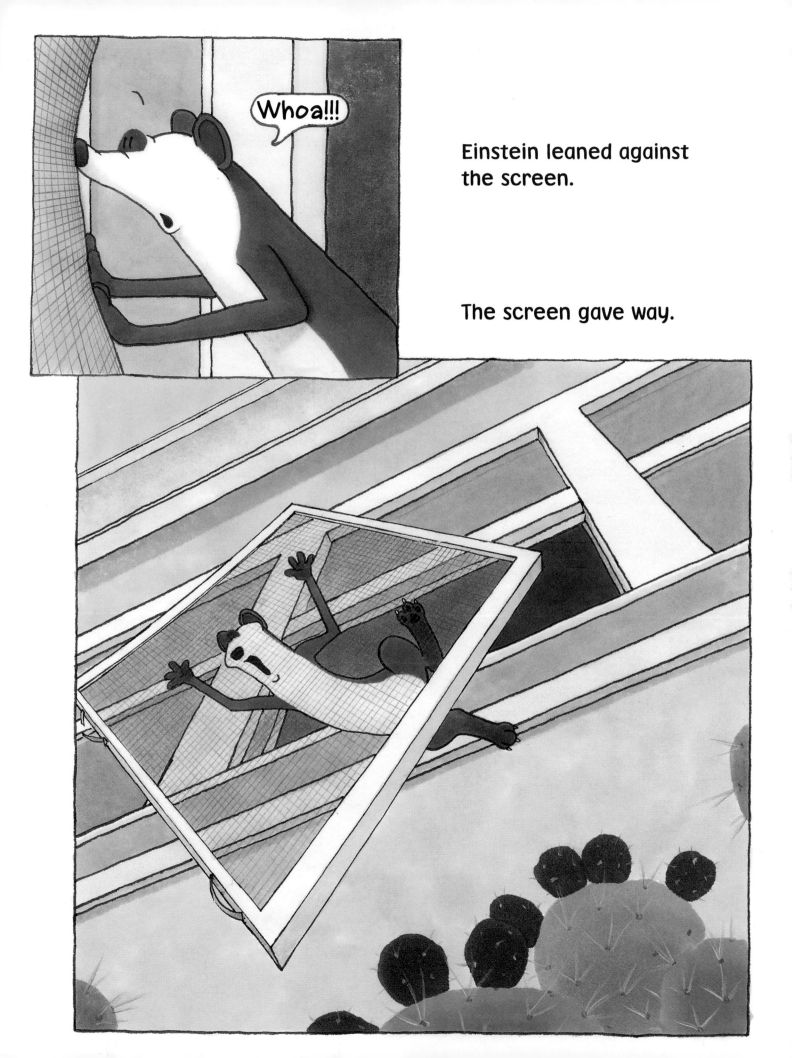

Einstein leaned against the screen.

The screen gave way.

Fudge closed his eyes and took a deep breath. Then he slunk
out of his hammock and scampered down the cage door.

He climbed up the sofa to the window ledge.

Then he looked down.

Fudge leaped to the ground.
He reached out to grab the
cactus fruit. . . .

Not so fast!

Einstein grabbed a chunk of
the cactus fruit and raced off.

Einstein stopped and waved the fruit at Fudge.

Einstein started running. Fudge chased him
up and down hills until he couldn't run anymore.

Fudge looked around. Nothing looked familiar.

Einstein sniffed around.

They raced up and down the hills
until they reached the ranch.

Then they scampered up the screen onto the window ledge,

down the sofa,

and straight toward their cage.

Einstein locked the cage door behind them—just in case.

Just then Andrea came back into the room. "It's time for us to go outside to explore. I brought your leashes."